From fingertips..

By Eue Poetic

From her lips

I drink the waters..

Calling forth the fountain of youth.

Sip the moisture, drink me in..

True love has been imbued.

Take a sip, drink me in she says

Love me in every which way..

Days go by, weeks, months, years

She beckons and calls, sipping away

All of my fears..

No more tears

Only love

Hold me dear.

Your heart,

Oh your heart is so beautiful..

it's like making love

To the sky itself.

You are more than a dream

Honey sweet,

When it's just us two..

Forever to hold,

Forever to cherish,

Deep inside of me.

Beauty, you see..

Is the projection of one's self

Onto the ordinary

Yet it is not so ordinary

When you behold such perfection.

Perfection in one so beautiful

That the sky no longer holds the key

To my heart..

The stars a mere twinkle..

When I think of you

The worlds collide

And galaxies fall forth,

Falling from our hearts..

My soul,

Your soul..

Tantalizing the universe

With passion,

Overwhelming the senses

bringing me to the peak.

Softly like the breeze,

Sweet like a honey bee

Flying through the flowers

For hours beneath the trees..

You whisper things that enthrall

Calling my soul

To grow, grow, grow..

Grow like a flower

You complete me

Completing my essence

As I sit here

Amidst my thoughts..

Such soft thoughts softly drifting

Through the cosmos.

Whispering, always whispering

Like the softest wind..

You enthrall me

Call me what you will

But this is just how I feel..

I feel your soul

Wandering through these galaxies of me,

Eternally,

Endlessly loving me..

Love..

Such a soft word

Said with the heart

Thought with the soul..

One word,

One smile..

Deep in these crevices of me

Love..

The best

Feeling

In

The

entire

World..

Love with all of you

It is what life is all about..

Thoughts often flow

Thoughts often grow

They grow like flowers

As i fall like snow..

It could never be cold in my heart

Not with you there,

Oh, these memories of your every smile..

I yearn..

I yearn for more,

A curve of your lips,

A kiss..

Anything that brings me closer

To you..

I long for a hug

From your arms,

Embrace me..

My heart races

When you trace my face

Leaving me so happy,

Tracing my soul

As you swim within me..

My soul flourishes

It flourishes!!

My soul must dance in mystic colors

Of the arcane..

When you sing to me,

My eyes light up like flames

My body a matchstick

Bursting to thoughts of you..

Sing to me..

Sing to me of the future

A future with you.

The road is long in this life,

Hell, we all know that..

There are a lot of shadows along the way

But no shadow

Could ever cross your face..

Not the way I see it,

You are beauty,

The very embodiment of it.

You are the light,

The sun,

The beauty that I wish to become..

Poetry on the lips of every poet,

You are the breath of the wind

With kisses that were blown into it,

And it is with you that I wish to sit..

The best thing about you,

You are alive,

So alive..

So alive with life..

There couldn't be anything better than that.

Not to me..

I almost feel crazy,

Crazy about you..

Insane with this love that I feel

Blahhhhhhhhhhhh!!!

Do I sound crazy?!?

If love is crazy, then I am insane beyond the comprehension of the human race..

That's what I feel for you.

I think I always will..

I love you.

I love loving you,

You are so very special..

There must be

Butterflies in my soul

In my veins even

It's as if at any moment I could fly away..

I would fly away with you,

Any day..

Twice on Friday.

On a soft breeze, softly fluttering

With a sing song tune

Playing in the background of my soul..

With a soft drizzle

This drizzle that fills me

With so much love..

If your voice would rain down on me

In hail and ice,

I wouldn't complain..

I would just know that I need

To start acting sane.

Rain down on me.

Pour your love on me,

Pour it on thick

Pour it on with every grin

Just give me those lips..

Can I have a sip?

No, not of your drink..

Just one sip of your lips!!

One sip of your smile

Because that is what makes these butterflies flit..

I will cherish you

Cherish you so strongly

That you will forever be a part of me..

For just one smile,

I will love you eternally..

Smile daily,

And I will give you all of me.

No doubt, that mouth is just like heaven.

Flowing like water,

Warm like the sun,

Beautiful like sunshine,

Heavenly like the angels above..

You are gorgeous..

All that you are..

And you will forever be in my heart.

In this cage of ribs

My heart do beat

To a tune of you,

A symphony ever so sweet..

Thoughts, feelings, emotions..

Are but a mere drop in the ocean,

Oh this commotion that you set in motion

The day you gave me that smile

Like some kind of love potion..

Thunder, Lightning

that's what comes when you aren't around

And it is so very frightening..

Where the clouds are loud

But i find you in the lost and found.

I would drown without you,

I am found when I am with you

Under the moon, the sun, the stars

I just want to be where you are..

I just want you to love me

The way I love you

For eternity..

Perfection,

Rejection,

Perfect rejection

that's all I've ever known

Until i met you..

You hold me when I am near

Nearer to you than ever before

Our love everlasting,

But i want to love you more..

Always more..

I could never love you enough.

I have always been rejected

Rejected by nobody you,

Nobody could ever be you

Or do what you do..

Or be everything that you are

To me.

On heavenly wings,

You ride the wind..

On heavenly wings

You deny my sins..

On heavenly wings,

You bless me with a grin..

On heavenly wings,

You bring me home..

On heavenly wings

I am never alone..

On heavenly wings,

Your voice so soft..

On heavenly wings,

You found me when I was lost..

On heavenly wings,

You bring me light..

On heavenly wings

You feel so right..

You are beautiful darling,

that's all I'm saying..

Even when you frown,

Nah, I'm not even playing.

In the ocean, in the sea,

Under the stars, here with me..

In the mountains, in the rain,

Full of hope, in the suns rays..

I could love you, I think I will,

But I have to wonder, how does that make you feel?

I see stars in your smile,

Beauty never forgotten,

How could I ever forget

Something that makes me so smitten?

You are beautiful darling,

You will always be..

Long after I am gone, into eternity..

You are so divine

That I'm sure you are made of butterflies

Made of sunshine

And everything bright..

You are so beautiful

That flowers must grow in your smile,

I know they grow in your soul..

You are so divine

That constellations form in your heart

At the heart of you where it can never be dark..

You are so very warm

Your smile is like being in a butterfly swarm

Or being witness to a lightning storm,

You are a force of nature..

Divine femininity,

Like the smile of a little honey bee,

So sweet, at least to me..

Never let me go,

Never let me die

Never hold my hand

And then say goodbye..

Never let my heart beat alone

Never stop being my home..

Just never let me go.

Be mine forever

No yandere

Just be mine!!

Never let me go,

Never say goodbye,

Never say goodnight

Without turning out the light..

I love you..

I wish,

I wish..

My 11:11 wish is that you smile today

That the universe brings you a sunrise

As beautiful as your soul.

Because I think that might make your heart smile

Just a tad, just a bit,

And then I wish that I could give those lips a kiss..

If I could kiss you right now

I would kiss your soul..

Simply because there is nothing more beautiful.

I have fallen in love with you

Like every good book I have ever read

I fall in love with your voice every day

And everything that you have ever said..

I have fallen in love with you.

Take my shadows

Make them gold

Take my darkness

And I am sold..

Take my heart

And make it yours

kiss my soul

Then take me on the floor..

hear my voice

And make it soft

Make my heart even softer

And I will love you lots..

Take my path

And leave me falling

Into you

Where heaven is calling..

I am nothing but a honey bee

Lost in your honey, my sweet Queen

Dreaming of heavenly smiles

Upon your face so eloquently..

I am nothing but a little dove

Falling further in love, my Queen

Dreaming of your beauty

For there is nothing as sweet..

You know what the bee said about making honey??

He said it was a pretty sweet job!!

It's about as sweet as making you smile..

I want to bring the woman out of you

To caress those softer parts

Caress smiles onto your skin with these lips

Speaking poetry until your heart is full

And your face smiles with glee..

Heaven,

It's not a place..

It's a time.

It's when we are together..

Hell can be any number of things,

But this one thing I know,

You are the light in my life.

You are beautiful

You are wonderful

You are amazing

You are lovely

You are smart

You are funny

You are fun

You are intelligent

You are creative

You are so many things,

But ugly is not one of them..

Never that.

Start off the day right!!

Start it with an, 'I love you' to your person..

That can be any number of things,

You can say good morning,

Bring them a cup of coffee,

Tell them their hair looks nice when it's messy..

You can say it in any number of ways, just thinking about them first thing in the morning says I love you in a way that can't be bought.. no flowers will ever say I love you like a morning ritual.

I love you in the morning first,

And then I drink my coffee..

I think of you first,

And then I wake up..

That's how the morning should go!!

Good morning love,

Here's your coffee..

there's a sticker on it that says I love you

If I could see what your heart does

When you smile,

I think that would be the most beautiful thing..

Does it speed up to thump again?

Does it twitch just a little bit?

Does it tense up or relax?

I wonder what your heart does

When you smile?

I know mine beats a little faster

When you smile..

When you smile

It lights up the room

it's so beautiful,

Almost like the moon..

But I think it's closer to the sun

Because just like Icarus

I fell madly in love..

If you could look into me

You would be mesmerized,

Why?

Because you would see your own eyes.

I think about them a bunch.

Oh yeah, can I take you to lunch?

If you could look into my soul

You would see your own,

Why?

Because we are soulmates,

ain't that great? Maybe that's why

I'm always thinking of your eyes.

If I could look into your mind

What would I find?

Would it be a picture of me?

What would it be?

Would there be a flurry of thoughts?

Or would I just get lost?

She was every part of me

And every part of herself

She was every part of me

Even though you couldn't tell..

She was two parts heaven

And one part hell.

Forget what you knew

You transcend all of that,

Your soul was made to grow

To heaven and back..

With wings you fly

Not in the sky silly

Like an angel you soar

Ya feel me??

You are a creature of the light

A soul quite like sunshine

that's why you live in the light

Because you seek heavens might

And if things don't feel quite right

Maybe you need to get out of the dark

Get closer to heaven

And let it in your heart..

Forget about the past

You transcend all of that

It was made to learn from

Let it fade to black..

With wings you fly

But not when you are high

That gets you low

Closer to hell but it feels like sky..

You aren't a creature

You are a human bean

that's why you live in the light

And that's why you live free

If things don't feel quite right

You need a change

Get closer to heaven

And spread your wings..

You understand me,

You tempt me to make me a better me

A stronger me..

You want to see good things for me,

To instill a positive change,

And that is priceless

Because not everyone has my best interest in mind.

that's the crazy thing about the world,

Not everyone does.. but you do and that makes a difference.

To me.

It means the world to me.

Just thank you, so much.

I appreciate you

And I am so grateful for you.

Soft thoughts

Softer still,

Almost falling from the window sill

Taking away my pain,

Is this window pane?

Taking from me

Everything..

Dreams, some say

But no dreams

Can sing a song

So beautiful..

Still, they are soft thoughts

Softly breezing my mind

Consuming my time

And slowly taking

My life..

Dream of me,

Oh, dream of me..

Every thought,

Every second

Of every day..

Sleep next to me

This sweet infatuation

Take my hate

And decapitate it

don't leave me..

don't leave me dilapidated.

I could love you

I think I can, i think i can

Hold out your hand

Can you understand?

I am a man

That means I am damned.

Damned if I do,

Damned if i don't..

I love you

Like nothing in this world

I can prove it

I will stand by your side

I will love you all of my life

Every day

And every night..

Heaven and hell

Are two completely different things

But angels don't kiss and tell

Only weeping within dreams..

    Within dreams..

    Within dreams..

Let that sink in.

Angels think in dreams.

They think so deeply

They are on a whole other conscious level

Often times weeping

For this world which rebels..

Tears fall like rain

In the heavens above

And where the droplets hit

The earth is covered in love..

Love is the answer..

She mesmerizes

There is a fire in her eyes

Like a mother lion..

Mother nature,

Divine femininity..

And when she cries

The earth shakes,

It quakes beneath me..

She never lies

Only lying next to me

Like the wind..

An eternal sin

Divine femininity..

When she sings

The birds sing too

Making music for you..

Divine femininity..

Without you

My life would be in shambles

Life is already a gamble

I couldn't imagine it without you..

If there were a world without you,

I would never want to live..

It would be a hopeless place,

A world with an evil face.

Life with you

Is a life filled with love,

You couldn't imagine

How much you fill me with love.

Or maybe you could,

Maybe that was your plan

To make me fall in love

Holding your beautiful hand..

With you embedded

I could never dread it,

This life that I live..

If heaven is where I'm headed.

That place with you

Heaven sent from above,

An entire realm of possibilities

Of endless love..

Life with you

Is a life filled with love,

You couldn't imagine

How much I want to give you a hug..

Or maybe you want one

Just as bad,

Possibly to take away

Every time you have ever been sad.

In your embrace

My heart races..

It erases all that I'm facing,

Like my heart is dancing

it's prancing like a deer in winter

Trying to get away from the cold

But that's not really it,

I want to be close to you

Down to my soul..

Nobody is like you,

Nobody is as nurturing,

No one cares so much

if I am hurting..

    Deep inside

    So deep..

I hurt sometimes,

I do..

    But I would hurt so much more

    Without you.

        The pain is sometimes greater

          Than the whole,

            It seems..

          I feel like a fool,

        My soul a primordial pool of pain..

But its's ok.

it's not ok but i am. I have you.

In my soul,

I drink you in

Just a sip

From your intoxicating lips..

I spill not a drop

As this ink drips.

In my heart,

I hug you tight

I squeeze the life out of you

And it just feels right..

I hurt you naught

Caught in your light.

In my mind,

I think about you always

In all ways

All day..

And all I can say is, damn!!

Jumbo hugs

Gigantic kisses

With 30 or so I love you's

Always mixed in..

that's the recipe for a delicious night

I want to treat you right,

Give you everything

You want..

Just so hopefully you'd grace my dreams,

And haunt me in delicious ways..

Let me kiss your face..

I love your taste.

Now if I could just get your recipe for cookies

Then I would be set!!

Give me some of that yummy goodness,

Ummmm, yeah!!

I

Could

Love you

Forever and

A day plus a little

Bit of always mixed in..

I could love you forever

Mixed with a smile

Plus two hugs

And a bit

Of you..

<3

Forever and Always..

Drinking her divine juices

Like they are life itself..

Every breath, created just for this..

Every touch, a fire within

Every caress of my fingertips

Seeking flame and sweat,

Shivers, quivers, quakes..

I think yes, life was created for this.

That desire, that passion..

That hunger as it grows

Like an addiction,

Because I am so addicted to her.

Carnal hunger within

Please take me now,

I can't live without her touch..

Fire within dancing with sin.

Caverns of beauty

Mountains of affection

Skies full of stars,

Oh, to think of natural selection..

To think this could all exist by accident

Is the saddest thought..

To think that we were all accidents

And that nobody loves us..

That we are all alone.

That really is the saddest thought..

The universe is great enough to create

Such wonderful things as life

And people choose to believe that we were accidents,

All of those beautiful creatures

Mountain views and sunrises bursting with colors,

How could that be an accident.

I choose to believe..

I am nothing but a bag of bones

With a meat sack wrapped around

And in 20 -30 years or less,

I will be dumped in the ground..

Not to think dark thoughts,

I am filled with love..

All I really need now is Ohhhh

About twenty three billion hugs..

Feelings compound feelings

And they drown out reality

I sit here and wonder

what is wrong with me..

Can I ever be loved?

Will I ever be enough?

am I destined to walk this world

With it being so rough?

Life is more beautiful than ever

With you by my side..

How could I ever forget you?

You know that I love you, right?

You fill my every waking hour,

You are the love of my life..

I need you here with me now,

Never leave me alone.

You are my home away from home,

No, you are my home..

And I love you dearly,

Stay here with me.

You are my best friend,

Before I met you,

I wished that my life would end..

But you changed all that.

Thank you for being you,

I love you so much..

I appreciate your existence more than you know.

All

I

Ever

Wanted

And

Needed

Was

A

Friend

And

I

Found

It

In

You..

Beautiful, it's a word to describe so many things.. but my favorite of all is you. You are the epitome of beauty, and you transcend even that. I would go as far to say that you are the most beautiful thing to have ever existed, a perfection that simply can't be beat.. nothing will ever take that away from you.

Sunshine explodes in my veins

When you smile..

Galaxies form in my eyes,

I become a celestial being

Of untold love,

And to my surprise..

I fall endlessly.

Now I know how Icarus must have felt,

Flying into the sun,

But i don't have wings..

I'm just standing here watching you smile

And I feel like my heart is on fire.

Falling, falling, fell..

Oops!! i fell in love..

Sunshine.. it grows towards things.

Just as I grow towards you..

Reaching out as if to touch you,

Reaching out for your embrace.

I can feel the sunshine

On my skin when you smile,

it's so pristine..

I can feel it deep inside of me.

I saw this sign that said for a deeper,

Fuller pout, inject our sauce in your lips..

Seriously, I was like wtf?? who would

Want that? haha.. if you smiled, I won!

I only want your smiles,

they beam beauty into my life..

that's something i could use more of,

Every single day!!

Friends like you last a lifetime

You want to know why?

Because you are true to yourself first,

Meaning you can be true to others..

Like be true to me,

that's all that I ask..

I don't know how that's such a hard task

For some of these people.

Be honestly you, don't be your friends

don't do what they do..

Think for yourself

And be true to you.

If you can do that, well then..

You will fit in my life just fine,

I don't have room for fakes

In my life..

You know?

don't you agree?

don't you?

Through the darkness

I see the light

A smile peeking through

Fleeting night..

Your smile brings me so much joy

It takes away the night in my soul,

Your smile brings the sunrise

And it helps me to grow..

Your heart must have a thousand galaxies

Teeming with life,

Starlight, star bright

Love, thoughts of you fill my nights..

Beauty is often sought with makeup

Often sought by exercise

Rarely these days

Is it found behind a pair of eyes..

Beauty, you see?

Is not just what you see..

Beauty can be

In just about anything.

Beauty can be inside too

Inside you..

Beauty can be red

Or beauty can be blue.

Beauty can be a smile

Or beauty can be a heart..

Beauty can be the sun

Or beauty can be the dark.

Beauty can be a mind

Or beauty can be a dream..

Beauty can be you

Or beauty can be me.

If your lips

Were any hotter

They would be a flaming ball of plasma..

When we kiss

i'm out of breath

Just like I have asthma..

Hold my hand

And dance with me

Forever and a day..

Two plus two

Equals four

At least that's what they say..

I say

Me plus you

Equals a family.

An angel couldn't make a sound

Sweeter than your laugh..

A bird couldn't make a song

Sweeter than you sound.

Sounding so delicious

Never vicious

Such simplistic reality

The way you sound to me..

You are like a prayer

Like a dream..

So soft

But never fleeting.

As you swarm my thoughts

Like drops of rain

I am consumed with you

No longer feeling my pain..

Do you know how I feel?

Can you feel it too?

I love how it feels like to be with you..

You are the softest flame

Warming my heart,

You are so soft..

The softest of the soft,

And i love you lots.

You have the most beautiful name

Lighting up the stars,

You are so hot..

The hottest of the hot,

And i love you lots.

there's no love

Like your love,

there's nothing

More beautiful than your love..

I love you lots,

So much..

Galaxies swirl in your soul

Where your warmth warms me

Like ten thousand suns

Of pure love..

Stars as far as the Milky Way

Grace the space between us

That consume with me with

The essence of love..

These constellations

Of sweet desire within

Elate me with each and every grin

That defies mystery..

Galactic winds of fire

Oh this sweet desire within

To seek out your smile

For all of history..

Six thousand years

Would not be long enough,

This love in my heart

Proves to be almost too much..

I love you like a beautiful view

Taking you into me,

In my mind you dine

On the sweetest parts of me..

You are the mountains,

You are the trees..

You are the birds,

And you are a breeze.

I love you like the sky is blue

Even when it is red,

Pinks and purples in the perfect hue..

Just know that my love is true.

You are so beautiful,

You don't even know how much so

With smiles like sunshine,

it's no wonder why flowers grow..

Your smiles warm the bones,

In your words I find a home,

And even when I sleep at night..

I could never truly feel alone.

From fingertips

Every wish come true,

Bringing me closer to heaven..

Bringing me closer to you.

If there were no one out there

There would be no reason for stars

There would be no reason for worlds beyond

If we were alone

The universe would be gone..

It would just be blackness all around

In the darkness we would drown

I like to believe

I believe..

In a power greater than me,

That addiction can be won,

Like listening to your favorite song,

From fingertips to souls so strong,

Looking up at the moon all night long,

How could this all be an accident?

How could we live?

How could we be?

How could there be a you?   How could there be a me?

All of my life..

I have searched far and wide

For a sign..

I have reached beyond

In every song

Lain awake at night

Fighting addiction

After addiction

Only to find..

That I won't find bliss

In any addiction

Except my addiction

For you..

it's simple

I love you

And I would do

Just about anything

For you..

Fire, brimstone

The flames upon your lips

With every kiss

Drips with eternal bliss

As it blossoms

Like a flower

Of untold arcane power..

Such subtle fire

Of passionate desire

Within is sired

And I grin..

Sweet kisses are the bliss

Of a thousand centuries

Every kiss within your lips

I know were meant for me..

Every word you speak

A flower that grows inside

Like a blooming grace

As beautiful as your face..

Sweet serenity

Explodes within me

And i just know that

You will be with me always..

Serendipity!!

A sweet surprise

Knowing you..

I love you..

Your heart

Etched with the sweetest honey..

Like your name,

Stitched with sunshine.

In your eyes

I see a billion stars

Lighting up my world

A beacon in the dark..

A honey bees smile

Filled with thick, raw honey

Could never be as sweet

As the dreams you bring to me..

Honey!!

Such a sweet thing

Knowing you..

I adore you..

Wait for me

On the other side of death

With a warm hand

Outstretched..

As I pass through the gates

Of endless death

Caress my soul

And show me what comes next..

Usher me into that place

With a warm smile

And bring me to the brink

Of an endless sunrise..

No sunsets

This is just the beginning

There is no end

To love..

Death is not the end

My friend,

don't be afraid..

There is no end

To the days..

There will always be more

Lives to live.

It may not be you

And it may not be me

But we will be there

Happily..

Our souls will swim

Without sin or evil

There is no devil

Worse than those inside us

Once we are gone they will be dead..

Your heart is golden

Like the finest honey to eat

If I could eat your heart,

I would think..

Sweeeeeet!!

What a delectable treat!!

A heart like honey

Just for me..

You say the sweetest things

All for me..

And i can't help but to love you

To the moon and back

I will be the big spoon,

And lay against your back..

Such beauty in an act

Like a smile..

Such beauty in an act

Like kindness..

Such beauty in an act

Like love..

Love is the most beautiful thing

Like loving you while we swing

Legs swinging beneath..

Love is precious

Love is grand

Love is lending a hand

When no one else will..

Love should splash, splatter, and spill..

Your voice could command army's

But it just commands my heart

And I think that's a really good start

Command this desire within me

This craving to be blessed by your smile..

I crave you,

I need you,

I adore you,

I implore you..

Smile for me.

When you smile,

My life feels complete

In that moment

Every second that your lips curve upward

Is a world of its own

And own me it does

With the greatest love..

I love the way you laugh,

I adore the way you think..

You bring me to the brink

Of ecstasy..

it's an aphrodisiac

Being this close to you

And i can do nothing but swoon..

Whispers that enthrall

Those little whispers in bed

The ones where you kiss my neck

With so much love..

          When we cuddle away the days

Safe from the suns rays..

Warm under blankets

God, it leaves me dismayed..

This display of affection

Mmmmmmm, it really hits me in the heart..

Those whispers that enthrall

The way you make me fall

Effortlessly,

The way you make me feel weightless

Like a helium balloon

No longer faceless

So in love with you..

Your laugh is like champagne bubbles

In my soul,

Such endearing intoxication..

If I could cork your throat

I would save you for later

And drink you in as the sands of time fall

Like my heart does timeless eternal.

You had my heart

The first time you smiled..

It wasn't even a question.

You hold my soul

In the palm of your hand..

that's not a question either.

You sip from the waters

Of my essence like a creek..

Which was cold until your warm lips touched me.

From the very first moment

That very first inkling..

You had me.

You have me.

i'm stuck on you..

I can't get you out of my mind

I wouldn't want you out.

I need you.

Hopefully you need me as much.

I could love you

Always and everything that means

I could love you

Through it all and everything..

I could love you

Forever and even more

I could love you

Only you for evermore..

I can love you and I do..

Such softness

Softly caressing my soul

Making me feel bliss

As you drip your fingertips across my skin..

My soul reacts

To your laugh

As if it has always been a part of me

And i revel in it..

A kiss shared between us

A touch, a tap, just a bit of love..

Your laugh must have been sent

From above..

Heaven sent, lend me your hand

I wish to hold it until your hair is gray..

My 11:11 wish is for you to be happy today..

She likes her books,

She loves to laugh..

Spends her time in libraries

Because that's where it's at..

She likes her wine,

She loves her shows,

And when she gets undressed

Well, you'll never know..

She's the sweetest girl

The sweetest in the world

she's got a smile that drips galaxies

For the whole world to see..

She doesn't seem to be beautiful

At first glance

But take a second take

And you are like damn!!

I see her though..

I see a universe of perfection

Everything that I have always desired

She is a thousand worlds of sunsets

Setting the night on fire..

        I see her always..

Setting my life ablaze with such beauty..

                    You are so sweet!!

                    Like a dream, I would say

                    And i was just wondering if

                    You would have coffee with me today?

                    I may not be the best looking

                    But my heart is golden

                    here's my hand

                    Would you like to hold it?

            I see you sitting there..

                    Looking as beautiful as can be

                    Like a dream, if i don't say..

And i was just wondering if

You would like to smile today?

I got you..

Would you set my day ablaze with perfection?

Send me a song

Send me a playlist that describes you..

Let me hear your soul in music form.

I want to know you

there is no better way..

I want to get deep inside your heart

Through your soul,

See what you see, feel what you feel..

I want to share those smiles,

Feel your pain..

I want to know you.

I couldn't make it through the day without you

Without your smile in my life?

I couldn't!!

i'm trying to hold onto you

Hanging on for dear life..

I could kiss your smile

Because it just feels so right.

If loving you were wrong, then doom me to hell..

I will love you through it all

As I fall, as I fall..

But it just so happens that your smile

that's heaven,

Loving you brings me closer to you

An angel..

A goddess..

So beautiful that i can't even explain.

Days without you are filled with rain.

Poetry is uttered with the heart,

It is one of life's finest arts..

Stars not withstanding

Poetry is the souls understanding.

Poetry was spoken

Every time that I said your name

Filling my heart with so much love

A heart that could never be tamed..

Poetry is forgotten

On the lips that never speak

Of a love that is forever

Between you and me..

Poetry soothes the soul

Drinking it like the fountain of youth

Bringing me closer to you..

True love is a love that defies time

A love that has a rhyme

that rhyme is a soulmate

And a soulmate has no expiration date..

You can find solace in poetry

Because maybe, those were your mates too

Birds of a feather flock together

When the poetry reaches you..

In an age of wonder

The wonders are never explained

it's like being thirsty

And then it starts to rain..

it's unexplainable

that's all i'm saying..

The wonders never cease

With beauty in every lane.

SHe's sweet like molasses,

Thick, yummy..

Kind of like clown,

But only because she's funny.

She's sexy like a librarian,

Oooh throw her against the books,

The way she wears her glasses,

she's just got that look..

And just like books,

She deeper than she looks

She wears sexy well,

But she'll steal your heart like a crook!!

How did I get to be so lucky?

How did you get to be so beautiful?

These questions go hand in hand

Because you have me falling like a fool..

i'm just the jester

Here to make you smile

If i didn't know any better

i'd say you have the perfect style..

I just want you to know

That i am so grateful for you

You don't realize that you came into my life

At just the perfect time..

You are always there

With a kindness that can't be beat

And i want you to know,

That it is so truly sweet..

Seriously,

It is.

Falling forever

Falling for you

Falling out of my shoes

When we are together

I choose you

Why?

Because i'm falling for you..

You are so endearing to me

      The way you touch my soul

            The way you touch my heart

So softly, such soft hands..

  Soft, softly touching me

      I wouldn't have it any other way..

    I wouldn't dream of it.

    How did you enamor me so completely?

      How did you come into my life so suddenly

  And take such control over my thoughts?

i'm not complaining though,

            I love it so much.

      I love you so much.

You are the epitome of perfection..

Her heart is like an ocean

So deep and filled with life

A vast sea of darkness

That lights up with every sunrise..

Just like her soul is like the moon

So bright in a sea of darkness,

A beacon of light to light the way

For all travelers of night.

But she is more like the sun,

Such brightness and glee

Simple perfection

Lighting the way for me..

Truth is, she's a force of nature

Quite unlike anything

But mirrored in everything

Perfection at its finest

Poetic in nature

She is poetry..

You are so beautiful,

I just wanted you to know that..

What do you call a romantic tree?

Sappy!!

Smile today, even if it's in your heart..

Sobriety is the hardest thing in the world

When you are an addict..

But if you really want to quit,

you'll get there..

Just take it day by day,

don't lose hope,

And reduce the amount that you use

Fight through the pain,

Try to stretch the amount of time between uses

And don't forget that you want to quit..

It sounds easy when it's put like that

But I assure you,

it's the hardest battle you will ever fight..

Seek help if you need it,

And you will need it,

People care..

There is a fire in your soul,

I can feel it..

Reach out to me

Touch my soul in ways

That I could only dream of..

Touch me so deeply

That my soul resonates

Vibrates

And reaches back..

I wish to have your fire

Inside of me too,

I wish to be a part of you..

Sweetness

Your lips are sweetness

Your smile is greatness

Your laugh is beautiful

Your thoughts are wonderful

You are amazing..

Repeat it..

My lips are sweetness

My smile is greatness

My laugh is beautiful

My thoughts are wonderful

I am amazing..

Now live it..

Those are your affirmations of the day.

You are amazing, you are..

And you are so truly beautiful.

You are a perfect, imperfect perfection just by being you..

She's like a good book,

Deep, thick, amazing,

And you never know

What adventure awaits..

You are beautiful, beautiful, beautiful, beautiful, beautiful, beautiful, beautiful, beautiful, beautiful, beautiful, beautiful, beautiful, beautiful, beautiful, beautiful, beautiful, beautiful, beautiful, beautiful, beautiful, beautiful, beautiful, beautiful, beautiful, beautiful, beautiful, beautiful, beautiful, beautiful, beautiful, beautiful, beautiful,

beautiful, beautiful, beautiful, beautiful, beautiful, beautiful,
beautiful, beautiful, beautiful, beautiful, beautiful, beautiful,
beautiful, beautiful, beautiful, beautiful, beautiful, beautiful,
beautiful, beautiful, beautiful, beautiful, beautiful, beautiful,
beautiful, beautiful, beautiful, beautiful, beautiful, beautiful,
beautiful, beautiful, beautiful, beautiful, beautiful, beautiful,
beautiful, beautiful, beautiful, beautiful, beautiful, beautiful,
beautiful, beautiful, beautiful, beautiful, beautiful, beautiful,
beautiful, beautiful, beautiful, beautiful, beautiful, beautiful,
beautiful, beautiful, beautiful, beautiful, beautiful, beautiful,
beautiful, beautiful, beautiful, beautiful, beautiful, beautiful,
beautiful, beautiful, beautiful, beautiful, beautiful, beautiful,
beautiful, beautiful, beautiful, beautiful, beautiful, beautiful,
beautiful, beautiful, beautiful, beautiful, beautiful, beautiful,
beautiful, beautiful, beautiful, beautiful, beautiful..

Oh, I'm sorry.. this room echoes when the truth is being told.

Thinking about you

Is the best part of my day,

Thinking about your smile

Makes my day..

And when you smile

My day almost breaks,

A sunrise shines

And my legs shake..

I think about you often

Often times wondering

How you could be so

Truly splendid..

Honey thick,

Honey sweet

I think

You are just right for me..

You are a honey bees dream

With that smile like honey,

So truly sweet

I can't even think..

If i could have you all to myself

I wouldn't spill a drop

I would take you into me

And love you lots..

You are everything that I crave

A honey bee would pollinate your grin

.Just be brave

Because i am going to kiss your chin..

Honey fire

Drizzles from my heart

Like galaxies of endearment

Lofting to the heavens..

Constellations of utter love

Oh, to be loved by another

So deeply that the stars

Become my lover..

Angels fall

Angels fly

Angel tears

Make angels cry..

Drip these galaxies from me

Let them fall from my lips..

Catch every star with yours

As i give you this kiss.

Dream of me, where art thou

The sweetest smile from your mouth

couldn't be a sweeter kiss..

As i take a bow

Stars fall out

Oh, to feel such bliss..

Simple smiles without complexity

Every word falling softly into me

A laugh bubbles within..

Simply bringing me to the brink

Of your sweet eternity

Without the weight of sin..

Forevermore, forevermore

To explore the reaches of your mind

Forevermore, forevermore

Through space and time..

Be my Juliet

From whence love came

I will be your Romeo

But that's not my name..

I will write you sonnets

Songs and sweet poetry

If you would just sit

Right here with me..

I will love you dashing

Gnashing on your lapel

Licking your boots

And savoring your smell..

I will love you something uncanny

Living the dream

Sitting with you until dark

Whispering sweet things..

You are like fire

Licking at the back of my mind

The sweetest desire

That life could ever bring alive..

You are the flames

You are the fire

You are the passion

Of untold desire..

You are heat

You are wind

You are the sea

When the waves begin..

You are the happiness

That i seek within..

You are divine femininity..

Goodnight dearest,

Sleep with the angels

Because your smile,

That belongs in heaven..

Thank you for reading this poetry book!! It means the world to me that you actually gave it a chance.. you are beautiful to me. Don't let the world be too hard on you. I'm sure you are hard enough on yourself.

Just remember that you are a beautiful soul. So perfectly you in your imperfect ways. Nobody could ever be you, that's why you exist.. because only you can be you. So be you!! Be beautiful in ways that only you can.

I hope that this book brought you a smile or two, maybe made you think.. and until next time, keep smiling!!

Eue Poetic..